A NOTE TO PARENTS ✎ W9-AXW-366

Reading Aloud with Your Child

Research shows that reading books aloud is the single most valuable support parents can provide in helping children learn to read.

- Be a ham! The more enthusiasm you display, the more your child will enjoy the book.
- Run your finger underneath the words as you read to signal that the print carries the story.
- Leave time for examining the illustrations more closely; encourage your child to find things in the pictures.
- Invite your youngster to join in whenever there's a repeated phrase in the text.
- Link up events in the book with similar events in your child's life.
- If your child asks a question, stop and answer it. The book can be a means to learning more about your child's thoughts.

Listening to Your Child Read Aloud

The support of your attention and praise is absolutely crucial to your child's continuing efforts to learn to read.

- If your child is learning to read and asks for a word, give it immediately so that the meaning of the story is not interrupted. DO NOT ask your child to sound out the word.
- On the other hand, if your child initiates the act of sounding out, don't intervene.
- If your child is reading along and makes what is called a miscue, listen for the sense of the miscue. If the word "road" is substituted for the word "street," for instance, no meaning is lost. Don't stop the reading for a correction.
- If the miscue makes no sense (for example, "horse" for "house"), ask your child to reread the sentence because you're not sure you understand what's just been read.
- Above all else, enjoy your child's growing command of print and make sure you give lots of praise. *You are your child's first teacher — and the most important one. Praise from you is critical for further risk-taking and learning.*

— Priscilla Lynch
Ph.D., New York University
Educational Consultant

Text and illustrations copyright © 1997 by Hans Wilhelm, Inc.
All rights reserved. Published by Scholastic Inc.
HELLO READER! and CARTWHEEL BOOKS and associated logos
are trademarks and/or registered trademarks of Scholastic Inc.

Library of Congress Cataloging-in-Publication Data

Wilhelm, Hans, 1945-
    I am lost/ by Hans Wilhelm.
        p.   cm.— (Hello reader! Level 1)
    Summary: A little dog gets lost and learns to find his way home again.
    ISBN 0-590-30699-5
    [1. Dogs — Fiction.   2. Lost children — Fiction.]   I. Title.
II. Series.
PZ7.W64815Iaf   1997
[E] — dc21   96-54158
                                                                    CIP
                                                                    AC

                    10 9 8 7 6 5 4 3 2 1

                    Printed in the U.S.A.   24
                    First printing, November 1997

I AM LOST!

by Hans Wilhelm

Hello Reader! — Level 1

SCHOLASTIC INC.
New York Toronto London Auckland Sydney

Oh, what a pretty leaf!

I must catch that leaf.

Come here, leaf.

I got you!

Where am I?

Oh, no! I am lost.

I want to go home.

I need help!

I know what to do.
I'll find a police officer.

Please help me, Officer.

I am lost.

Here is my address.

This is my street.

I am home again.

Thank you, Officer.